# THE
# SULLIVAN COUNTY SKETCHES
# OF STEPHEN CRANE

# THE
# SULLIVAN COUNTY
# SKETCHES
## OF
# STEPHEN CRANE

*Edited, and with an introduction, by*
MELVIN SCHOBERLIN

*Illustrations by*
GEORGE VANDER SLUIS

SYRACUSE UNIVERSITY PRESS

FIRST EDITION

93479

*For*
**KERSTEN**
*in remembrance of*
16 July 1937
*and other days*

# CONTENTS

# INTRODUCTION

"How I wish I had dropped them [*The Sullivan County Sketches*] into the wastebasket! They weren't good for anything, and I am heartily ashamed of them now, but every little while someone rakes them up and tells me how much pleasure he had from reading them—throws them in my face out of compliment." Stephen Crane, in this manner, and from the vantage of 1896, apparently banished forever his "Sullivan County Sketches" (seven of which are here published for the first time in book form). Yet by so doing, he also renounced his first measure of success as a writer of fiction. Neither one nor the other, however, could he disassociate from the New York *Tribune*, where, indeed, most of the tales had first appeared. To his mind both newspaper and sketches had become inexorable symbols of a most inglorious defeat—a rout which, after 1892, forever closed to him the columns of *The Tribune*. Against him subsequently, when the publication of *The Black Riders* and *The Red Badge of Courage* had brought him fame if not fortune, this journal directed its interminable and frequently pointless attacks. Crane, in spite of the deep wounds suffered by his sensitive nature, kept silent; yet the rancor remained. The bitterness of his judgment then, we can assume, resulted more from these attacks than from considered criticism. For his first-published stories, however, there endured affection: in July of 1895 he had urged their publication as a book to Copeland and Day. Yet, to Lily Brandon he wrote: "Can you not send them to me? . . . There is no one in the world has any copies of them but you."

But Crane balanced right and error in his estimate of their importance. Not one of the Sullivan County Sketches is a great short story; at times they are inconsequential and juvenile. Nevertheless, it is equally clear that several fulfill their author's purpose, and all are important as examples of fiction written during the transitional period when Stephen Crane was evolving a method and style which ignored, for the most part, the fictional standards so generally accepted in the 1890's and made possible the creation of *Maggie, The Black Riders,* and *The Red Badge of Courage.* Here, too, are illustrated, potentially at least, the singularities of style, method, and point of view for which Crane was later to be so indiscriminately praised and so maliciously condemned by critics on both sides of the Atlantic. These sketches, moreover, were inextricably associated with the incident which was to change the direction of his life as a writer.

Eighteen ninety-two was the great turning point of Crane's career. He was twenty, and had quite "recovered from college," which he had abandoned in disgust the previous year; his future as a journalist seemed almost secure. Although several of the big Eastern dailies had been publishing his press articles and resort correspondence since 1887, the present optimistic state of affairs had resulted only after considerable manipulation on the part of his brother Townley, manager of a news bureau in the New Jersey resort of Asbury Park. Willis Fletcher Johnson, day editor of *The Tribune,* a not inconsiderable purchaser of the bureau's weekly "gabble," was, it so happened, summer vacationing at the Park. Not only had he been one of Dr. Jonathan Townley Crane's students during the ten years that Stephen and Townley's father was President of Pennington Seminary but he later became an intimate of the abundant family that made up the Crane household.

Townley had often urged his younger brother to show some of his best stories to the editor. But Stephen was reluctant, not so much from lack of confidence in his work as from fear that what he wrote might be misunderstood—or even worse, ignored. So, following Townley's explanation of the situation, the editor sent for Stephen and asked to see some of the stories.

But young Crane was, nevertheless, considerably more worldly than his fellows at twenty, and certainly more experienced than this account would indicate. For even as a boy, when he wandered ragged and hungry along the streets of Port Jervis and Asbury Park while his mother lectured brilliantly on Woman's Rights or Temperance at Boston, Nashville, Chicago, or along the Jersey Coast, his existence had been carefree, and his experiences remarkable in their variety.

Yet this serves rather to exaggerate the negative facets of Crane's childhood. An opposing, integrating element was injected into these early years by his elder sister Agnes, upon whom, at fifteen when Stephen was born, largely devolved the responsibility and care for not only her youngest brother but for the entire household as well. A brilliant, exacting student and teacher, severe in demeanor, politely revolutionary, and painfully sensitive of her plainness—"my mother's ugly duckling" she characterized herself in her journal—an affectionate girl who desired, first of all, to be (yet in accordance with her own definition) a "Christian lady" and, then, "to *write*." But at length writing to her became most important of all, while there were times when she admitted that she was something less than a "Christian lady." Upon Stephen, until her death at twenty-eight in 1884, she lavished her boundless affection and understanding. And more than anyone else, it was she who gave direction to his early years. She taught him much of literature and science, and of living; she directed, to a great extent, his reading. With enthusiasm and deep pride she looked upon his childish stories and poems. Like his sister, Stephen was sensitive and moody and often rebellious. In the midst of "such an oyster-like family," as she summed up the household, a strong bond developed between the two rebels. And like her, his outlook on life was inordinately serious.

Never was he to be happier than during these early years. There were long tramps with his Newfoundland retriever Solomon over the wild, rugged hills beyond Port Jervis—the scene so faithfully described in *The Sullivan County Sketches*—and later there were the bareback travels on his circus pony Pudgy from Asbury Park south as far as Shark River, where he loved to stretch full length on the grassy shores and contemplate lazy fish in the black pools. But the elements of nature were so construed in him that, growing restless and lonely, he hurried his small steed back to the Park and soon lost himself in the crowds that swept along the boardwalk. From the solitude of the hills and the river; from the horses and dogs (which were to him the most understanding of all living creatures); and lastly, from the boiling mobs that surged along the boardwalk of the Park in summer or the crowds that scurried frantically through the streets of Easton, Syracuse, and New York City in winter— from these he knew many things.

But of the rapaciousness of man and of the injustices of a civilized society he had yet much to learn as he sprawled beside Willis Johnson on the veranda of the West End Hotel in June of 1892. Stephen had still to face the appalling economic problems of living—problems for which, indeed, he was never able to determine satisfactory solutions during his brief life. Consequently he had not yet been exposed to that final bitter phase of education which was to solidify his youthful amorphous ponderings into a philosophy of desperate naturalism. Among the manuscripts which he passed without comment to the older man, nevertheless, were at least fragments of a short novel which he had written in the Delta Upsilon House at Syracuse University and which was later to be published as *Maggie: A Girl of the Streets*. Within nine months Crane was himself to print this naturalistic exposé of social injustice, but at that moment the fate of *The Sullivan County Sketches* was of more immediate concern. Not only would their acceptance broaden his wedge in journalism but it would also translate into reality his ambition to write of those things which he found important or interesting in a manner that was personally satisfying. And so the young man awaited the older man's decision.

"I was very favorably impressed," Johnson has written of the incident, "and at once accepted them for use in the Sunday supplement of *The Tribune*."[1] It was agreed that Crane would receive the regular space-rate of six dollars a column. "Four Men in a Cave," the first of the sketches to be used, was published July 3, 1892. Appearing on succeeding Sundays were "The Octopush," "A Ghoul's Accountant," "The Black Dog," "Killing His Bear," and several miscellaneous press articles. "A Tent in Agony," published in the December issue of *The Cosmopolitan Magazine*, marked Crane's debut into the circle of the big monthlies. And shortly thereafter, Henry Phillips, then editing *The University Herald* for the Delta Upsilon Chapter at Syracuse University, requested a contribution from his former classmate. "The Cry of A Huckleberry Pudding," which

---

[1] I have extracted this quotation by Willis Fletcher Johnson, together with those that follow, from "The Launching of Stephen Crane," *The Literary Digest International Book Review*, IV (April, 1926), pp. 288-290. To avoid spotting these pages with unnecessary footnotes I refer to that periodical any reader further interested in Editor Johnson's version of the *Tribune* episode; nevertheless, I wish to make evident the fact that Wilbur, Edmund, and William Crane, that Arthur Oliver, Post Wheeler, Frederic M. Lawrence, Ralph Paine, Hamlin Garland, Louis Senger, Corwin Linson, Mrs. Elizabeth H. Richards—each a friend or a member of Stephen's family—have given unequivocal evidence that Townley and Stephen were discharged by *The Tribune*. M. S.

appeared in the *Herald* for December 23rd, was the last of the
Sullivan County Sketches to be published during Crane's life.

In spite of the fact that his sketches and press articles now
found a ready market with *The Tribune*, Crane continued,
throughout the summer, to cover the coast resorts in search of
news items for Townley's weekly column "On the New-Jersey
Coast." And Townley, more often than not, was quite content
to let his younger brother write the column. Circumstances,
then, were certainly not unique when, on August 20th, while
Townley fished for pickerel at the Hartwood Club, Stephen
wrote the *Tribune* "gabble," surveying the social events of the
previous week. Clearly, the most important of these had been
the American Day parade by the New Jersey councils of the
Junior Order of United American Mechanics. This organization
of artisans, once so powerful, is today practically unknown.
Aligned with no party, and only obliquely political, its primary
aims were "to restrict immigration, and to protect the public
schools of the United States and to prevent sectarian inter-
ference therein . . . . We are bound together to promote Ameri-
cans in business and shield them from the depressing effects of
foreign competition. We are not a labor organization, nor are we
a military company."

The account of the JOUAM parade, then, became the lead
paragraphs. But Crane, already becoming deeply conscious of
the social and economic injustices suffered by the workingman,
was piqued by its perfect irony, at once so plain to him but of
which everyone else, apparently, was oblivious. The style—
bitter, ironic, and ruthless in its social criticism, yet with a
probing penetration of basic values—is stark Crane. An origi-
nality and frankness of this variety was neither anticipated,
suitable, nor acceptable in the pages of a conservative Republican newspaper. Nevertheless, on Sunday, August 21, 1892,

New Yorkers, upon opening their *Tribunes* to page 22, read:

Asbury Park, N. J., Aug. 20 (Special).—The parade of the Junior Order of United American Mechanics here on Wednesday afternoon was a deeply impressive one to some persons. There were hundreds of the members of the order, and they wound through the streets to the music of enough brass bands to make furious discords. It probably was the most awkward, ungainly, uncut and uncarved procession that ever raised clouds of dust on sun-beaten streets. Nevertheless, the spectacle of an Asbury Park crowd confronting such an aggregation was an interesting sight to a few people.

Asbury Park creates nothing. It does not make; it merely amuses. There is a factory where nightshirts are manufactured, but it is some miles from town. This is a resort of wealth and leisure, of women and considerable wine. The throng along the line of march was composed of summer gowns, lace parasols, tennis trousers, straw hats and indifferent smiles. The procession was composed of men, bronzed, slope-shouldered, uncouth and begrimed with dust. Their clothes fitted them illy, for the most part, and they had no ideas of marching. They merely plodded along, not seeming quite to understand, stolid, unconcerned and, in a certain sense, dignified—a pace and a bearing emblematic of their lives. They smiled occasionally and from time to time greeted friends in the crowd on the sidewalk. Such an assemblage of the spraddle-legged men of the middle class, whose hands were bent and shoulders stooped from delving and constructing, had never appeared to an Asbury Park summer crowd, and the latter was vaguely amused.

The bona fide Asbury Parker is a man to whom a dollar, when held close to his eye, often shuts out any impression he may have had that other people possess rights. He is apt to consider that men and women, especially city men and women, were created to be mulcted by him. Hence the tan-colored, sun-beaten honesty in the faces of the members

of the Junior Order of United American Mechanics is expected to have
a very staggering effect upon them. The visitors were men who possessed principles.

In these three paragraphs Stephen Crane launched, not too
wisely perhaps, the first attack of his personal war, pursued
relentlessly and fearlessly so long as he lived, against social and
moral injustice. (Furthermore, it is noteworthy that the major
part of what he wrote subsequently lay somewhere within his
plan for this conflict.) To the modern reader the irony and the
direction of his attack are clear. Not so in 1892! The New York
press ignored the matter; not so the New Jersey newspapers!
They protested violently, and the reactions of the Asbury Park
journals were, understandably, the most venomous of all—BUT
for the wrong reasons. An immediate retraction of the article
and an apology to the JOUAM was demanded by *The Daily
Spray*, which reprinted the original article in full. *The Asbury
Park Journal*, in a bitter attack on everyone who might con-
ceivably have been connected with the incident, concluded:

It is said that the *Tribune's* regular letter-writer, J. Townley Crane,
was engaged on something else last week, and delegated the task of
writing the usual Sunday gabble to another. This young man has a
hankering for razzle dazzle style, and has a great future before him if,
[un]like the good, he fails to die young. He thought it smart to sneer at
the Juniors for their personal appearance and marching . . .

But when national politics were finally injected into the situation, with sallies directed against Whitelaw Reid, owner and
publisher of *The Tribune*, the entire affair assumed a ludicrous
importance. During the previous spring Reid had resigned his
post as United States Minister to France to enter politics, and,
following the Republican convention in July, he campaigned
vigorously with President Harrison, as its vice-presidential

nominee. To avoid the mixing of diplomacy and politics with journalism he had long since relinquished—though exercising, no doubt, his prerogative to dictate its general policies—the active editorial control of his paper. Furthermore, during Crane's indiscretion Reid had been stumping in the Middle West.

The year, thus far, had been a singularly disastrous and turbulent one for both labor and business. Strikes in the mines of Idaho and Pennsylvania, on the railroads, in the steel mills, the Homestead riots and the so-called Pinkerton massacre, the mustering of the state militias and the United States Army to protect private property—all had contributed to a profound national unrest. The *Tribune* staff, as a result, faced a particularly difficult task in navigating the paper through the political narrows during an election year. Its policies, conservative and rigid, collaborated to make its position, if not quite untenable, at least decidedly uncomfortable where labor was concerned.

It becomes readily apparent that Crane's ironical correspondence, through misinterpretation, rendered the paper still more vulnerable to the attacks of labor, although it did not, as some individuals have said, tilt the November election returns in favor of Grover Cleveland. Up to this point Editor Johnson sets down the facts correctly. Moreover, he establishes the *Tribune* incident as being the turning-point in Crane's career, for, more than anything else, it forced him from news-reporting into the field of fiction. Of the succeeding events, however, in which he assumed an important (but certainly a less commendable) role, the editor says nothing. "I was," he admits, "the day editor of *The Tribune*, and all such news-correspondence came under my direct and sole charge . . . Practically all of that early work of . . . [Crane's] was done under my direction and was published under my editing." Yet Crane's literary flight brought notoriety—and swift retribution. Both he and Townley were summarily discharged by *The Tribune*—a fact which Johnson denies emphatically; nevertheless, the members of the Crane family, who were in a position to know, have agreed that such was indeed the case. Townley, however, had little difficulty in clearing himself of blame and was soon reinstated; but for Stephen, after the articles which had already been accepted were published, the columns of *The Tribune* remained forever closed.

Furthermore—and *this* is the point which Johnson chooses to ignore—when Stephen himself later became news, *The Tribune* let escape no chance, and indeed often manufactured opportunities, to attack, malign, and extirpate him. In one item of many in a similar vein the paper said, among other things equally uncomplimentary, "It does not appear to us that the modern era owes anything at all to Mr. Crane and his likes, anything save half-baked essays in work which it were idle to call either prose or verse, anything save weariness unspeakable." To his old friend Louis Senger, who had called to his attention this particular bit of vituperation, Crane wrote, "Hope you will keep me posted on the Tribune's acrobatics."

Nevertheless, so profound was his bitterness about the *Tribune* incident, and so violent were his reactions when questioned concerning it, that the subject was generally recognized by his friends as taboo. Through the pages of this paper, however, he had achieved three things—he had won at least a measure of recognition, he had discovered a reliable market for short fiction and press articles written in a manner not without satisfaction to him, and he had established himself as a young journalist with good prospects for the future.

All three were washed away by the publication of the JOUAM paragraphs. And not until two years later, when, under the sponsorship of William Dean Howells and Hamlin Garland, the New York *Press, The Arena,* and the Bacheller and McClure syndicates opened to him their columns, was he able to recapture the position which he had achieved so easily in 1892. Of course any conjecture as to the direction Crane's career might have pursued had circumstances been altered would be pointless; nevertheless, there are conclusions which appear not unsatisfactory. For him the interlude between victory and victory was years of unrelieved defeat and profound disappointment, of hunger and patched clothes and a worn gray ulster, of sleeping wherever he might discover friends (usually young artists or internes who, like himself, perceived the depression, possessed of little more than ambition and an exuberant confidence in themselves, their work, and the future) who were satisfied and able to share with him a bed, a sofa, or a suitable coalbox.

Yet they were years of achievement, too. For Crane learned many things from the lives that encircled his own. His notebooks overflowed with observations of tramps and men of affluence and power, of whores and social darlings. Life was indeed to him a text vital and more interesting than either *Bell's Vowel Table* or Welsh's *Development of English Literature and Language.* He worked hard and wrote unceasingly, carefully, confidently. *The Red Badge of Courage,* written during this interlude, "was an effort born of pain, and I believe," he commented later, "that was beneficial to it as a piece of literature." It was with sad resignation, nevertheless, that he at length accepted the proposition made so painfully clear to him: "that art should be a child of suffering." And life, he concluded, wore the complexion of sorrow:

Brevity is an element that enters importantly into all pleasures of life, and this is what makes pleasure sad. And so there is no pleasure, but only sadness.

Yet from a cloth woven of sadness, revolt, and anarchy he created *The Black Riders*.

For the intimate friends of Stephen Crane the first of *The Black Riders'* "lines" came with appalling abruptness. Poetry, rarely the subject of his animated conversations, as far as Corwin Linson, Louis Senger, Frederic Lawrence, Lucius Button, Nelson Greene, and Hamlin Garland were aware, had just not been included in the catalog of Crane's literary interests. Of the Victorian poets, however, he made apparent his singularly low opinion. Each of his friends, together with a new member of the circle, John Barry, was strangely impressed by the haunting "lines," for which they, with one exception, acknowledged no precursor in American literature. But following Crane's death in 1900, Barry, grasping at relationships as at straws in a direction where, indeed, none existed, said (and his error has been echoed, with a few noble exceptions, by two generations of biographers and literary historians): "It was plain enough to me that they [*The Black Riders* poems] had been directly inspired by Miss Dickinson. . . . And yet, among all the critics who have discussed the book, no one, to my knowledge at any rate, has called attention to the resemblance between the two American writers." Although there is common to their poems an element of revolt, the men who ate, slept, and worked with Crane during the years when he was "turning on and off the poetic spout" have agreed that the work of Emily Dickinson neither inspired nor influenced *The Black Riders* or *War Is Kind*. And those critics who have discovered in these books echoes of Walt Whitman are somewhat nearer to the truth. But the conception of Crane's poems need concern us here no further than to direct the reader's attention to certain elements in *The Sullivan County Sketches* that foreshadowed his "lines." [2]

[2] A full-length biography of Stephen Crane, which I now have in preparation, will discuss this problem more fully. M. S.

Nevertheless, had critical insight been a property of the members of the Crane circle, they might readily have recognized that his fiction was often more nearly poetry than it was prose.

Even in his earliest Asbury Park correspondence and press articles we find the image of poetry frequently replacing the image of prose—if, of course, the reader recognizes the existence of such a boundary. It is strange, too, that critics have not explored this subject further (but jaded historians and critics were similarly affected with blindness in the case of *Moby Dick*), for much of *The Red Badge of Courage* is written in free verse without, of course, the identifying verse patterns. Of significance, however, are these fragments from *The Sullivan County Sketches*. From "Killing His Bear," for example, these lines:

> On the ridge-top a dismal choir of hemlocks
> crooned over one that had fallen.
>
> .  .  .  .  .  .  .  .  .  .  .  .  .  .  .  .  .  .
>
> A gray, ponderous stillness
> came heavily in the steps of the sun.

Or we may proceed a step farther with the opening lines of "A Ghoul's Accountant," with this result—the line divisions are, of course, purely arbitrary:

> In the wilderness sunlight is noise.
> Darkness is a great, tremendous silence,
> Accented by small and distant sounds.
> The music of the wind in the trees
> Is songs of loneliness, hymns of abandonment,
> And lays of the absence of things
> Congenial and alive.

From these it is but a little, little way to the free verse patterns of *The Black Riders*.

And not too remote from a consideration of these "lines" would be a very brief examination of Crane's unique employment of adjectives—especially those of color. Where a man perceived in nature only the monotonous gray of spinning colors ("You don green spectacles before you look at roses"), Crane's acutely sensitive eyes detected regiments of pure colors. For him "each small gleam was a voice . . . in little songs of carmine, violet, green, gold—a chorus of colors." These he translated into the medium of language in much the same manner as Cézanne interpreted the color and light in nature on canvas. Indeed, to discover a similar projection of color into language we have to con the works of such French poets as Rimbaud, Baudelaire, Valéry, Jean Pellerin, and Max Jacob. And like them, or like Poe or Henry James, Crane often symbolizes mood and emotion in terms of color; yet, for him, color was but a primary advance into *le symbolisme*. Although in 1892 he was ignorant of both Impressionism and Symbolism in art and literature, four years later, nevertheless, he was the most important proponent of these two movements in American literature.

Crane observed color in nature through an artist's eyes. It was a faculty innate, an adverb of his genius. But in the absence of a patent explanation for this faculty, one apparently logical and easily acceptable has been coined. He, it has been said, learned to use color through his association, during the middle nineties, with the struggling artists who inherited the old studios of the Art Students League on 23rd Street. Here, it is true, the new French movements in art and literature, although understood only vaguely if at all, were violently debated; it is not unlikely that Crane whetted his perception and understanding of color on this stone. But from this group he borrowed nothing of his technique.

Color and light flood the pages of *The Sullivan County Sketches*. Therein appear 139 adjectives denoting color: gray-39, black-22, red-21, yellow-15, brown-11, white-7, green-6, blue-4, silver-2, orange-1, purple-1, and miscellaneous hues-10. But of his extraordinary technique in the employment of color adjectives (it was neither a trick, an affectation, nor a febrile straining for effect, for his conversation was even more colorful, brilliant, and sparkling with fresh word combinations than either his prose or poetry), Crane was not yet master. Still, we cannot fail to admire the facile imagery of such phrases as: "the torches became studies in red blaze and black smoke"; "swore great lurid oaths which blazed against the sky"; "a mass of angry, red coals glowered and hated the world"; "said the slate-colored man in a voice of somber hue"; "yellow famine was in his eyes"; "the dying sun created a dim purple and flame-colored tumult on the horizon's edge"; and "a gray, ponderous stillness came heavily in the steps of the sun."

"Ironical situations," John Galsworthy remarked in one of his rare interviews, "somehow, always appeal to me most. Why I cannot say." To such a point of view Crane would have nodded a characteristically animated agreement. For not only did irony appeal to him, but he made of it practically a hallmark. It is a design in the fabric of *The Sullivan County Sketches*. The final lines of "The Black Dog" and "A Tent in Agony" illustrate his peculiar employment of irony. And particularly do the last sentences of "Killing His Bear": "He ran up and kicked the ribs of the bear. Upon his face was the smile of the successful lover," anticipate still more famous lines: "The red sun was pasted in the sky like a wafer," and, from "The Blue Hotel," this: "The corpse of the Swede, alone in the saloon, had its eyes fixed upon a dreadful legend that dwelt atop of the cash-machine: 'This registers the amount of your purchase.' "

But while his irony might evoke from the reader an occasion-
al smile, it is sharply barbed, ruthless, and often devastating to
the singular egotisms of mankind. He examines the species with
profoundly cynical amusement. Furthermore, his humor is
somber, tempered by fear or terror, or overwhelmed by horror. In
"The Black Dog," at least, we detect a definite influence of
Ambrose Bierce, whose *Tales of Soldiers and Civilians* Crane had
read shortly after publication and admired. But even the Sullivan County Sketches, with their humorous situations and
amusing dialogue, are seldom "funny"; rarely do they provoke
a "belly-laugh." Of all Crane's work probably the most gen-
uinely amusing scene is in "The Carriage Lamps." Jimmie
Trescott, a small wayfarer of childhood, is confined, by way of
punishment, to his room. His pal, however, Willie Dalzel, alias
Hold-up Harry, the Terror of the Sierras, and chieftain of as
marvelous a band of juvenile assassins as ever extinguished a
foe in fiction, strenuously maneuvers to free the prisoner from
his "ex—excwable enemies." But at this particular moment
Jimmie's father, *the* "excwable enemy," enters the pirate's
prison, appraises the secret plans of escape; then, concealing
himself in the shadows, he commands the threatened, but now
desperately unwanted, rescue to proceed. —And it does.

Although Crane rarely permits his readers to savor the humor
in his situations, he frequently relieves the tension of horror by
balancing subject and treatment. "The Cry of A Huckleberry
Pudding," although certainly one of the least commendable of
the sketches, provides an interesting illustration. The terror of
the three men is alleviated for the reader somewhat when the
howls of the little man are described with such grotesque and
ponderous exaggeration: "The cry of the unknown instantly
awoke them to terror. . . . There was a pause which extended
through space. Comets hung and worlds waited. . . . Roars

went to the ends of the earth, and snarls that would appall
armies turned the men in the tent to a moaning mass with forty
eyes." The terror of the men becomes ludicrous. The intense and
real agony of the little man as he rolls on the ground, however,
is punctuated by the incongruously funny exclamations of "Oh,
thunderation!" In this story Crane makes the most—so much,
in fact, that it becomes distractingly dull—of a tragi-comic
situation.

A charge of slightness to a point of being inconsequential
might be directed, and not entirely without reason, against
most of these sketches; a similar charge might be leveled, also
with reason, at Henry James's *The Spoils of Poynton*. But the
fact remains that from each the reader emerges with a broader
knowledge and deeper understanding of human nature—even
though in *The Sullivan County Sketches* human nature never
gets very far. The egotism of the little man, however, is wonderful to behold.

As the central character of the sketches, it is his success or
failure that each records. Yet in only two of the stories, "The
Cry of A Huckleberry Pudding" and "Killing His Bear," does
he personally have a part in directing his destiny. Chance, or a
collaboration of natural events, or Nature—naturalism, if you
will—in the remaining stories determines the fate of the little
man and his companions. He, with them, escapes from the recluse in "Four Men in a Cave" only because, lacking further
funds with which to bet, he is unable to call the hermit's hand at
poker. The escape in "The Octopush" is effected through the
Individual's attack of delirium tremens. As the ghoul's accountant, he is doomed no matter what figure he stammers. The
black dog and death collaborate to sustain and confound his
contention. A flypaper salesman and circumstances trap the
little man, although he does get the last kick. The devil—

by chance cast in the role of a bear—makes a twin in "A Tent in Agony." The little man proceeds victoriously, but only because the "holler" tree, quite by chance, in falling, has smashed his companion's eggs. He swells detestably with power and success when, through no contrivance on his part, the mountain lies motionless at his feet. The little man, then, is as insignificant as the gambler in "The Blue Hotel," of whom Crane wrote: "This poor gambler isn't even a noun. He's a kind of an adverb."

The Sullivan County Sketches were contrived from fact. The four men were actual; they haunted the Sullivan wilderness each August from 1891 to 1896, exploring farther up the Mongaup Valley and deeper into the dense forests which covered the hills between Hartwood and Port Jervis, and fishing for pickerel from their favorite stumps in Pond Eddy. These tales record with fidelity, if not always real incidents, at least the quality of their adventures. The four men who tramped the Sullivan County miles together, Louis Senger has said, were cast as:

The Little Man................................Louis E. Carr, Jr.
The Pudgy Man........................Frederic M. Lawrence
The Tall Man................................Louis C. Senger, Jr.
The Quiet Man........................................Stephen Crane

The last two, of course, are never named in the sketches. They are, in fact, superfluous baggage. Crane bungles badly here. He had not yet learned to condense, to convey infinite meaning in a few swift, bold, precise strokes. And this quality in his work is an important element of his genius.

The chiefest importance, therefore, of *The Sullivan County Sketches* exists in the fact that they are the transitional pieces, dividing the work of Stephen Crane of the "college essay" and the uninspired resort gabble from that of Stephen Crane, genius.

And of this fact was Crane himself wholly aware. For to his beloved Lily Brandon he was to write on February 29, 1896:

You know, when I left you [shortly after the completion of these sketches], I renounced the clever school in literature. It seemed to me that there must be something more in life than to sit and cudgel one's brains for clever and witty expedients. So I developed all alone a little creed of art which I thought was a good one. Later I discovered that my creed was identical with the one of Howells and Garland and in this way I became involved in the beautiful war between those who say that art is man's substitute for nature and we are the most successful in art when we approach the nearest to nature and truth, and those who say—well, I don't know what they say. Than that they can't say much but they fight villianously and keep Garland and I out of the big magazines. Howells, of course, is too powerful for them.

If I had kept to my clever Rudyard-Kipling style, the road might have been shorter but, ah, it wouldn't be the true road. The two years of fighting have been well-spent. And now I am almost at the end of it. This winter fixes me firmly. We have proved too formidable for them, confound them. They used to call me "that terrible, young radical," but now they are beginning to hem and haw and smile—those very old coons who used to adopt a condescending air toward me. There is an irony in the present situation that I enjoy, devil take them for a parcel of old, cringing, conventionalized hens.

But in *The Sullivan County Sketches* a young though authentic new literary voice was raised. Yet their form and subject, if not their style, lay wholly within the familiar conventions of American realism. They were inspired, undoubtedly, by the boisterous, outdoor masculinity of the tall tales and Western humor of such writers as John Phoenix, M. Quad, Bill Nye, Petroleum V. Nasby, and Artemus Ward, and perhaps by the humorous sketches of his own mother, but especially by the realistic sketches of Mark Twain in *Roughing It* and *Life on the Missis-*

*sippi*. They were experiments in form and style. But the method finally evolved through the writing of these tales became basic for everything that Crane was to produce thereafter. Yet this method, here imperfectly displayed, when subsequently applied to more ambitious canvases, it should be remembered, signaled a definite break from *both* the romantic and realistic schools in late nineteenth-century American literature. Furthermore, the purpose of fiction was becoming more definite in Crane's own mind. As he later said: "I try to give the readers a slice out of life." And "a novel," he further explained, "to my mind, should be a succession of . . . clear, strong, sharply-outlined pictures, which pass before the reader like a panorama, leaving each its definite impression." With but little rewriting, the sketches in this book could easily be welded together into a single story similar in form to *Maggie* or *The Red Badge of Courage*. Or to reverse the process, we might quote an anonymous critic: " 'The Red Badge of Courage' which made Mr. Crane famous was not a sustained narrative, but a sequence of extraordinary tableaux."—And *this* was precisely Crane's design for the book.

*The Sullivan County Sketches*, then, were but trial flights in fiction—soarings in experiment that were to culminate in the creation of *The Black Riders*, *Maggie*, *The Red Badge of Courage*, *Whilomville Stories*, and "The Open Boat."

MELVIN SCHOBERLIN

Phoenix, Arizona
21 August 1948

# ACKNOWLEDGMENTS

My first obligation is to Mr. H. B. Collamore, who has placed at my disposal his collection of Stephen Crane manuscripts. I wish to thank Marchal E. Landgren for clarifying for me the involved relationships between the various movements in French art and literature during the nineteenth century. My other debts extend to the friends who have read or heard my Introduction, to Herbert F. West, Frederic M. Lawrence, E. A. Cross, Ames W. Williams, Corwin K. Linson, Max J. Herzberg, Edwin H. Cady, and Eleanor Schoberlin.

The texts I have reprinted, with the exception of "The Holler Tree" and "An Explosion of Seven Babies," where the original manuscripts have been used, are in each case that of the last published version for which Crane probably corrected the proofs. Spelling has been modernized, obvious typographical errors have been corrected, and a few minor corrections in punctuation have been made.

# THE
# SULLIVAN COUNTY SKETCHES

# FOUR MEN IN A CAVE

*Likewise Four Queens, and a Sullivan County Hermit*

THE moon rested for a moment on the top of a tall pine on a hill.

The little man was standing in front of the campfire making orations to his companions.

"We can tell a great tale when we get back to the city if we investigate this thing," said he, in conclusion.

They were won.

The little man was determined to explore a cave, because its black mouth had gaped at him. The four men took lighted pine-knots and clambered over boulders down a hill. In a thicket on the mountainside lay a little tilted hole. At its side they halted.

"Well?" said the little man.

They fought for last place, and the little man was over-whelmed. He tried to struggle from under by crying that if the fat, pudgy man came after, he would be corked. But he finally administered a cursing over his shoulder and crawled into the hole. His companions gingerly followed.

A passage, the floor of damp clay and pebbles, the walls slimy, green-mossed, and dripping, sloped downward. In the cave atmosphere the torches became studies in red blaze and black smoke.

"Ho!" cried the little man, stifled and bedraggled, "let's go back." His companions were not brave. They were last. The next one to the little man pushed him on, so the little man said sulphurous words and cautiously continued his crawl.

Things that hung seemed to be on the wet, uneven ceiling, ready to drop upon the men's bare necks. Under their hands the clammy floor seemed alive and writhing. When the little man endeavored to stand erect the ceiling forced him down. Knobs and points came out and punched him. His clothes were wet and mud-covered, and his eyes, nearly blinded by smoke, tried to pierce the darkness always before his torch.

"Oh, I say, you fellows, let's go back," cried he. At that moment he caught the gleam of trembling light in the blurred shadows before him.

"Ho!" he said, "here's another way out."

The passage turned abruptly. The little man put one hand around the corner, but it touched nothing. He investigated and discovered that the little corridor took a sudden dip down a hill. At the bottom shone a yellow light.

The little man wriggled painfully about and descended feet in advance. The others followed his plan. All picked their way with anxious care. The traitorous rocks rolled from beneath the little man's feet and roared thunderously below him. Lesser stones, loosened by the men above him, hit him on the back. He gained seemingly firm foothold and, turning halfway about, swore redly at his companions for dolts and careless fools. The pudgy man sat, puffing and perspiring, high in the rear of the procession. The fumes and smoke from four pine-knots were in his blood. Cinders and sparks lay thick in his eyes and hair. The pause of the little man angered him.

"Go on, you fool," he shouted. "Poor, painted man, you are afraid."

"Ho!" said the little man. "Come down here and go on your-self, imbecile!"

The pudgy man vibrated with passion. He leaned downward. "Idiot . . .!"

He was interrupted by one of his feet which flew out and crashed into the man in front of and below him. It is not well to quarrel upon a slippery incline when the unknown is below. The fat man, having lost the support of one pillar-like foot, lurched forward. His body smote the next man, who hurtled into the next man. Then they all fell upon the cursing little man.

They slid in a body down over the slippery, slimy floor of the passage. The stone avenue must have wibble-wobbled with the rush of this ball of tangled men and strangled cries. The torches went out with the combined assault upon the little man. The adventurers whirled to the unknown in darkness. The little man felt that he was pitching to death, but even in his con-volutions he bit and scratched at his companions, for he was satisfied that it was their fault. The swirling mass went some twenty feet and lit upon a level, dry place in a strong, yellow light of candles. It dissolved and became eyes.

The four men lay in a heap upon the floor of a gray chamber. A small fire smoldered in the corner, the smoke disappearing in a crack. In another corner was a bed of faded hemlock boughs and two blankets. Cooking utensils and clothes lay about, with boxes and a barrel.

Of these things the four men took small cognizance. The pudgy man did not curse the little man, nor did the little man swear in the abstract. Eight widened eyes were fixed upon the center of the room of rocks.

A great, gray stone, cut squarely like an altar, sat in the middle of the floor. Over it burned three candles in swaying tin cups hung from the ceiling. Before it, with what seemed to be a small volume clasped in his yellow fingers, stood a man. He was an infinitely sallow person in the brown-checked shirt of the plows and cows. The rest of his apparel was boots. A long gray beard dangled from his chin. He fixed glinting, fiery eyes upon the heap of men, and remained motionless. Fascinated, their tongues cleaving, their blood cold, they arose to their feet. The gleaming glance of the recluse swept slowly over the group until it found the face of the little man. There it stayed and burned.

The little man shriveled and crumpled as the dried leaf under the glass.

Finally, the recluse slowly, deeply spoke. It was a true voice from a cave, cold, solemn, and damp.

"It's your ante," he said.

"What?" said the little man.

The hermit tilted his beard and laughed a laugh that was either the chatter of a banshee in a storm or the rattle of pebbles in a tin box. His visitors' flesh seemed ready to drop from their bones.

They huddled together and cast fearful eyes over their shoulders. They whispered.

"A vampire!" said one.

"A ghoul!" said another.

"A Druid before the sacrifice," murmured another.

"The shade of an Aztec witch doctor," said the little man.

As they looked, the inscrutable face underwent a change. It became a livid background for his eyes, which blazed at the little man like impassioned carbuncles. His voice arose to a howl of ferocity. "It's your ante!" With a panther-like motion he drew a long, thin knife and advanced, stooping. Two cadaverous hounds came from nowhere and, scowling and growling, made desperate feints at the little man's legs. His quaking companions pushed him forward.

Tremblingly he put his hand to his pocket.

"How much?" he said, with a shivering look at the knife that glittered.

The carbuncles faded.

"Three dollars," said the hermit in sepulchral tones which rang against the walls and among the passages, awakening long-dead spirits with voices. The shaking little man took a roll of bills from a pocket and placed three ones upon the altar-like stone. The recluse looked at the little volume with reverence in his eyes. It was a pack of playing cards.

Under the three swinging candles, upon the altar-like stone, the gray beard and the agonized little man played at poker. The three other men crouched in a corner and stared with eyes that gleamed with terror. Before them sat the cadaverous hounds licking their red lips. The candles burned low and began to flicker. The fire in the corner expired.

Finally, the game came to a point where the little man laid down his hand and quavered: "I can't call you this time, sir. I'm dead broke."

"What?" shrieked the recluse. "Not call me! Villain! Dastard! Cur! I have four queens, miscreant." His voice grew so mighty that it could not fit his throat. He choked, wrestling with his lungs for a moment. Then the power of his body was concentrated in a word: "Go!"

He pointed a quivering, yellow finger at a wide crack in the rock. The little man threw himself at it with a howl. His erstwhile frozen companions felt their blood throb again. With great bounds they plunged after the little man. A minute of scrambling, falling, and pushing brought them to open air. They climbed the distance to their camp in furious springs.

The sky in the east was a lurid yellow. In the west the footprints of departing night lay on the pine trees. In front of their replenished campfire sat John Willerkins, the guide.

"Hello," he shouted at their approach. "Be you fellers ready to go deer-huntin'?"

Without replying, they stopped and debated among themselves in whispers.

Finally, the pudgy man came forward.

"John," he inquired, "do you know anything peculiar about this cave below here?"

"Yes," said Willerkins at once; "Tom Gardner."

"What?" said the pudgy man.

"Tom Gardner."

"How's that?"

"Well, you see," said Willerkins slowly, as he took dignified pulls at his pipe, "Tom Gardner was once a fambly man, who lived in these here parts on a nice leetle farm. He uster go away to the city orften, and one time he got agamblin' in one of them there dens. He went ter the dickens right quick then. At last he come home one time and tol' his folks he had up and sold the farm and all he had in the worl'. His leetle wife she died then. Tom he went crazy, and soon after . . . ."

The narrative was interrupted by the little man, who became possessed of devils.

"I wouldn't give a cuss if he had left me 'nough money to get home on, the doggoned, gray-haired red pirate," he shrilled in a seething sentence. The pudgy man gazed at the little man calmly and sneeringly.

"Oh, well," he said, "we can tell a great tale when we get back to the city after having investigated this thing."

"Go to the devil," replied the little man.

# THE OCTOPUSH

*A Sullivan County Nocturne*

Four men once upon a time went into the wilderness seeking for pickerel. They proceeded to a pond which is different from all other sheets of water in the world, excepting the remaining ponds in Sullivan County. A scrawny stone dam, clinging in apparent desperation to its foundation, wandered across a wild valley. In the beginning, the baffled waters had retreated into a forest. In consequence, the four men confronted a sheet of water from which there upreared countless gray, haggard tree trunks. Squat stumps, in multitudes, stretched long, lazy roots over the surface of the water. Floating logs and sticks bumped

gently against the dam. All manner of weeds throttled the lilies
and dragged them down. Great pine trees came from all sides to
the pond's edge.

In their journey, the four men encountered a creature with a
voice from a tomb. His person was concealed behind an enor-
mous straw hat. In graveyard accents, he demanded that he be
hired to assist them in their quest. They agreed. From a recess
of the bank he produced a blunt-ended boat, painted a very
light blue with yellow finishings, in accordance with Sullivan
aesthetics. Two sculls, whittled from docile pine boards, lay
under the seats. Pegs were driven into the boat's side, at con-
venient rowlock intervals. In deep, impressive tones, the dis-
guised individual told the four men that, to his knowledge, the
best way to catch pickerel was to "kidder fur 'em from them there
stumps." The four men clambered into the beautiful boat, and
the individual maneuvered his craft until he had dealt out to
four low-spreading stumps, four fishers. He thereupon repaired
to a fifth stump, where he tied his boat. Perching himself upon
the stump-top, he valiantly grasped a mildewed corncob between his teeth, laden with black, eloquent tobacco. At a distance it smote the senses of the four men.

The sun gleamed merrily upon the waters, the gaunt, tower-
ing tree trunks, and the stumps lying like spatters of wood which
had dropped from the clouds. Troops of blue and silver darning
needles danced over the surface. Bees bustled about the weeds
which grew in the shallow places. Butterflies flickered in the air.
Down in the water, millions of fern branches quavered and hid
mysteries. The four men sat still and skiddered. The individual
puffed tremendously. Ever and anon, one of the four would
cry ecstatically, or swear madly. His fellows, upon standing to
gaze at him, would either find him holding a stout fish, or nervously struggling with a hook and line entangled in the hordes

of vindictive weeds and sticks on the bottom. They had fortune, for the pickerel is a voracious fish. His only faults are in method. He has a habit of furiously charging the fleeting bit of glitter and then darting under a log or around a corner with it.

At noon, the individual corraled the entire outfit upon a stump, where they lunched while he entertained them with anecdote. Afterward, he redistributed them, each to his personal stump. They fished. He contemplated the scene and made observations which rang across the water to the four men in bass solos. Toward the close of the day, he grew evidently thoughtful, indulging in no more spasmodic philosophy. The four men fished intently until the sun had sunk down to some tree-tops and was peering at them like the face of an angry man over a hedge. Then one of the four stood up and shouted across to where the individual sat enthroned upon the stump.

"You had better take us ashore, now." The other three repeated. "Yes, come take us ashore."

Whereupon the individual carefully took an erect position. Then, waving a great yellow-brown bottle and tottering, he gave vent to a sepulchral roar.

"You fellersh—hic—kin all go—hic—ter blazersh."

The sun slid down and threw a flare upon the silence, coloring it red. The man who had stood up drew a long, deep breath and sat down heavily. Stupefaction rested upon the four men.

Dusk came and fought a battle with the flare before their eyes. Tossing shadows and red beams mingled in combat. Then the stillness of evening lay upon the waters.

The individual began to curse in deep maudlin tones. "Dern fools," he said. "Dern fools! Why dontcher g'home?"

"He's full as a fiddler," said the little man on the third stump. The rest groaned. They sat facing the stump whereon the individual perched, beating them with mighty oaths. Occasionally

he took a drink from the bottle. "Shay, you'm fine lot fellers,"
he bellowed, "why blazersh dontcher g'home?"

The little man on the third stump pondered. He got up finally
and made oration. He, in the beginning, elaborated the many
good qualities which he alleged the individual possessed. Next
he painted graphically the pitiful distress and woe of their
plight. Then he described the reward due to the individual if he
would relieve them, and ended with an earnest appeal to the
humanity of the individual, alleging, again, his many virtues.
The object of the address struggled to his feet and in a voice of
faraway thunder, said: "Dern fool, g'home." The little man sat
down and swore crimson oaths.

A night wind began to roar, and clouds bearing a load of rain
appeared in the heavens and threatened their position. The four
men shivered and turned up their coat collars. Suddenly it
struck each that he was alone, separated from humanity by
impassable gulfs. All those things which come forth at night
began to make noises. Unseen animals scrambled and flopped
among the weeds and sticks. Weird features masqueraded
awfully in robes of shadow. Each man felt that he was com-
pelled to sit on something that was damply alive. A legion of
frogs in the grass by the shore and a host of toads in the trees
chanted. The little man started up and shrieked that all creeping things were inside his stump. Then he tried to sit facing four
ways, because dread objects were approaching at his back. The
individual was drinking and hoarsely singing. At different times
they labored with him. It availed them nought. "G'home, dern
fools." Among themselves they broached various plans for
escape. Each involved a contact with the black water, in which
were things that wriggled. They shuddered and sat still.

A ghostlike mist came and hung upon the waters. The pond
became a graveyard. The gray tree trunks and dark logs turned

to monuments and crypts. Fireflies were wisp-lights dancing over graves, and then, taking regular shapes, appeared like brass nails in crude caskets. The individual began to gibber. A gibber in a bass voice appalls the stoutest heart. It is the declamation of a genie. The little man began to sob; another groaned; and the two remaining, being timid by nature, swore great lurid oaths which blazed against the sky.

Suddenly the individual sprang up and gave tongue to a yell which raised the hair on the four men's heads and caused the waters to ruffle. Chattering, he sprang into the boat and, grasping an oar, paddled frantically to the little man's stump. He tumbled out and cowered at the little man's feet, looking toward his stump with eyes that saw the unknown.

"Stump turned inter an octopush. I was asettin' on his mouth," he howled.

The little man kicked him.

"Legs all commenced move, dern octopush!" moaned the shrunken individual.

The little man kicked him. But others cried out against him, so directly he left off. Climbing into the boat, he went about collecting his companions. They then proceeded to the stump whereon the individual lay staring wild-eyed at his "octopush." They gathered his limp form into the boat and rowed ashore. "How far is it to the nearest house?" they demanded savagely of him. "Four miles," he replied in a voice of cave-damp. The four men cursed him and built a great fire of pine sticks. They sat by it all night and listened to the individual who dwelt in phantom shadows by the water's edge dismally crooning about an "octopush."

# A GHOUL'S ACCOUNTANT

*The Story of a Sullivan County Produce Deal*

In a wilderness sunlight is noise. Darkness is a great, tremendous silence, accented by small and distant sounds. The music of the wind in the trees is songs of loneliness, hymns of abandonment, and lays of the absence of things congenial and alive.

Once a campfire lay dying in a fit of temper. A few weak flames struggled cholerically among the burned-out logs. Beneath, a mass of angry, red coals glowered and hated the world.

Some hemlocks sighed and sung, and a wind purred in the grass. The moon was looking through the locked branches at four imperturbable bundles of blankets which lay near the agonized campfire. The fire groaned in its last throes, but the bundles made no sign.

Off in the gloomy unknown a foot fell upon a twig. The laurel leaves shivered at the stealthy passing of danger. A moment later a man crept into the spot of dim light. His skin was fiercely red and his whiskers infinitely black. He gazed at the four passive bundles and smiled a smile that curled his lips and showed yellow, disordered teeth. The campfire threw up two lurid arms and, quivering, expired. The voices of the trees grew hoarse and frightened. The bundles were stolid.

The intruder stepped softly nearer and looked at the bundles. One was shorter than the others. He regarded it for some time motionless. The hemlocks quavered nervously and the grass shook. The intruder slid to the short bundle and touched it. Then he smiled. The bundle partially upreared itself, and the head of a little man appeared.

"Lord!" he said. He found himself looking at the grin of a ghoul condemned to torment.

"Come," croaked the ghoul.

"What?" said the little man. He began to feel his flesh slide to and fro on his bones as he looked into this smile.

"Come," croaked the ghoul.

"What?" the little man whimpered. He grew gray and could not move his legs. The ghoul lifted a three-pronged pickerel-spear and flashed it near the little man's throat. He saw menace on its points. He struggled heavily to his feet.

He cast his eyes upon the remaining mummy-like bundles, but the ghoul confronted his face with the spear.

"Where?" shivered the little man.

The ghoul turned and pointed into the darkness. His countenance shone with lurid light of triumph.

"Go!" he croaked.

The little man blindly staggered in the direction indicated. The three bundles by the fire were still immovable. He tried to pierce the cloth with a glance and opened his mouth to whoop, but the spear ever threatened his face.

The bundles were left far in the rear, and the little man stumbled on alone with the ghoul. Tangled thickets tripped him, saplings buffeted him, and stones turned away from his feet. Blinded and badgered, he began to swear frenziedly. A foam drifted to his mouth, and his eyes glowed with a blue light.

"Go on!" thunderously croaked the ghoul.

The little man's blood turned to salt. His eyes began to decay and refused to do their office. He fell from gloom to gloom.

At last a house was before them. Through a yellow-papered window shone an uncertain light. The ghoul conducted his prisoner to the uneven threshold and kicked the decrepit door. It swung groaning back, and he dragged the little man into a room.

A soiled oil-lamp gave a feeble light that turned the pineboard walls and furniture a dull orange. Before a table sat a wild, gray man. The ghoul threw his victim upon a chair and went and stood by the man. They regarded the little man with eyes that made wheels revolve in his soul.

He cast a dazed glance about the room and saw vaguely that it was disheveled as from a terrific scuffle. Chairs lay shattered, and dishes in the cupboard were ground to pieces. Destruction had been present. There were moments of silence. The ghoul and the wild, gray man contemplated their victim. A throe of fear passed over him, and he sank limp in his chair. His eyes swept feverishly over the faces of his tormentors.

At last the ghoul spoke.

"Well!" he said to the wild, gray man.

The other cleared his throat and stood up.

"Stranger," he said, suddenly, "how much is thirty-three bushels of pertaters at sixty-four an' a half a bushel?"

The ghoul leaned forward to catch the reply. The wild, gray man straightened his figure and listened. A fierce light shone on their faces. Their breaths came swiftly. The little man wriggled his legs in agony.

"Twenty-one, no, two, six and . . ."

"Quick!" hissed the ghoul, hoarsely.

"Twenty-one dollars and twenty-eight cents and a half," laboriously stuttered the little man.

The ghoul gave a tremendous howl.

"There, Tom Jones, dearn yer!" he yelled, "what did I tell yer! hey? Hain't I right? See? Didn't I tell yer that?"

The wild, gray man's body shook. He was delivered of a frightful roar. He sprang forward and kicked the little man out of the door.

# THE BLACK DOG

*A Night of Spectral Terror*

THERE was a ceaseless rumble in the air as the heavy raindrops battered upon the laurel thickets and the matted moss and haggard rocks beneath. Four water-soaked men made their difficult ways through the drenched forest. The little man stopped and shook an angry finger at where night was stealthily following them. "Cursed be fate and her children and her

children's children! We are everlastingly lost!" he cried. The
panting procession halted under some dripping, drooping hemlocks and swore in wrathful astonishment.

"It will rain for forty days and forty nights," said the pudgy
man, moaningly, "and I feel like a wet loaf of bread, now. We
shall never find our way out of this wilderness until I am made
into a porridge."

In desperation, they started again to drag their listless bodies
through the watery bushes. After a time, the clouds withdrew
from above them, and great winds came from concealment and
went sweeping and swirling among the trees. Night also came
very near and menaced the wanderers with darkness. The little
man had determination in his legs. He scrambled among the
thickets and made desperate attempts to find a path or road.
As he climbed a hillock, he espied a small clearing upon which
sat desolation and a venerable house, wept over by wind-waved
pines.

"Ho," he cried, "here's a house."

His companions straggled painfully after him as he fought
the thickets between him and the cabin. At their approach, the
wind frenziedly opposed them and skirled madly in the trees.
The little man boldly confronted the weird glances from the
crannies of the cabin and rapped on the door. A score of timbers
answered with groans, and, within, something fell to the floor
with a clang.

"Ho," said the little man. He stepped back a few paces.

Somebody in a distant part started and walked across the
floor toward the door with an ominous step. A slate-colored man
appeared. He was dressed in a ragged shirt and trousers, the
latter stuffed into his boots. Large tears were falling from his
eyes.

"How-d'-do, my friend?" said the little man, affably.

"My ol' uncle, Jim Crocker, he's sick ter death," replied the slate-colored person.

"Ho," said the little man. "Is that so?"

The latter's clothing clung desperately to him and water sogged in his boots. He stood patiently on one foot for a time.

"Can you put us up here until tomorrow?" he asked, finally.

"Yes," said the slate-colored man.

The party passed into a little unwashed room, inhabited by a stove, a stairway, a few precarious chairs, and a misshapen table.

"I'll fry yer some po'k and make yer some coffee," said the slate-colored man to his guests.

"Go ahead, old boy," cried the little man cheerfully from where he sat on the table, smoking his pipe and dangling his legs.

"My ol' uncle, Jim Crocker, he's sick ter death," said the slate-colored man.

"Think he'll die?" asked the pudgy man, gently.

"No!"

"No?"

"He won't die! He's an ol' man, but he won't die, yit! The black dorg hain't been around yit!"

"The black dog?" said the little man, feebly. He struggled with himself for a moment.

"What's the black dog?" he asked at last.

"He's a sperrit," said the slate-colored man in a voice of somber hue.

"Oh, he is? Well?"

"He haunts these parts, he does, an' when people are goin' to die, he comes and sets and howls."

"Ho," said the little man. He looked out of the window and saw night making a million shadows.

The little man moved his legs nervously.

"I don't believe in these things," said he, addressing the slate-colored man, who was scuffling with a side of pork.

"Wot things?" came incoherently from the combatant.

"Oh, these—er—phantoms and ghosts and what not. All rot, I say."

"That's because you have merely a stomach and no soul," grunted the pudgy man.

"Ho, old pudgkins!" replied the little man. His back curved with passion. A tempest of wrath was in the pudgy man's eye. The final epithet used by the little man was a carefully-studied insult, always brought forth at a crisis. They quarreled.

"All right, pudgkins, bring on your phantom," cried the little man in conclusion.

His stout companion's wrath was too huge for words. The little man smiled triumphantly. He had staked his opponent's reputation.

The visitors sat silent. The slate-colored man moved about in a small personal atmosphere of gloom.

Suddenly, a strange cry came to their ears from somewhere. It was a low, trembling call which made the little man quake privately in his shoes. The slate-colored man bounded at the stairway and disappeared with a flash of legs through a hole in the ceiling. The party below heard two voices in conversation, one belonging to the slate-colored man, and the other in the quavering tones of age. Directly, the slate-colored man reappeared from above and said: "The ol' man is took bad for his supper."

He hurriedly prepared a mixture with hot water, salt, and beef. Beef-tea, it might be called. He disappeared again. Once more the party below heard, vaguely, talking over their heads. The voice of age arose to a shriek.

"Open the window, fool! Do you think I can live in the smell of your soup?"

Mutterings by the slate-colored man and the creaking of the window were heard.

The slate-colored man stumbled down the stairs, and said with intense gloom, "The black dorg'll be along soon."

The little man started, and the pudgy man sneered at him. They ate a supper and then sat waiting. The pudgy man listened so palpably that the little man wished to kill him. The wood-fire became excited and sputtered frantically. Without, a thousand spirits of the winds had become entangled in the pine branches and were lowly pleading to be loosened. The slate-colored man tiptoed across the room and lit a timid candle. The men sat waiting.

The phantom dog lay cuddled to a round bundle, asleep down the roadway against the windward side of an old shanty. The specter's master had moved to Pike County. But the dog lingered as a friend might linger at the tomb of a friend. His fur was like a suit of old clothes. His jowls hung and flopped, exposing his teeth. Yellow famine was in his eyes. The wind-rocked shanty groaned and muttered, but the dog slept. Suddenly, however, he got up and shambled to the roadway. He cast a long glance from his hungry, despairing eyes in the direction of the venerable house. The breeze came full to his nostrils. He threw back his head and gave a long, low howl and started intently up the road. Maybe he smelled a dead man.

The group around the fire in the venerable house were listening and waiting. The atmosphere of the room was tense. The slate-colored man's face was twitching and his drabbed hands were gripped together. The little man was continually looking behind his chair. Upon the countenance of the pudgy man appeared conceit for an approaching triumph over the little man, mingled with apprehension for his own safety. Five pipes

glowed as rivals of a timid candle. Profound silence drooped
heavily over them. Finally the slate-colored man spoke.

"My ol' uncle, Jim Crocker, he's sick ter death."

The four men started and then shrank back in their chairs.

"Damn it!" replied the little man, vaguely.

Again there was a long silence. Suddenly it was broken by a
wild cry from the room above. It was a shriek that struck upon
them with appalling swiftness, like a flash of lightning. The
walls whirled and the floor rumbled. It brought the men together with a rush. They huddled in a heap and stared at the
white terror in each other's faces. The slate-colored man
grasped the candle and flared it above his head. "The black
dorg," he howled, and plunged at the stairway. The maddened
four men followed frantically, for it is better to be in the
presence of the awful than only within hearing.

Their ears still quivering with the shriek, they bounded
through the hole in the ceiling and into the sick room.

With quilts drawn closely to his shrunken breast for a shield,
his bony hand gripping the cover, an old man lay with glazing
eyes fixed on the open window. His throat gurgled and a froth
appeared at his mouth.

From the outer darkness came a strange, unnatural wail,
burdened with weight of death and each note filled with fore-
boding. It was the song of the spectral dog.

"God!" screamed the little man. He ran to the open window.
He could see nothing at first save the pine trees, engaged in a
furious combat, tossing back and forth and struggling. The moon
was peeping cautiously over the rims of some black clouds. But
the chant of the phantom guided the little man's eyes, and he at
length perceived its shadowy form on the ground under the
window. He fell away gasping at the sight. The pudgy man
crouched in a corner, chattering insanely. The slate-colored

man, in his fear, crooked his legs and looked like a hideous Chinese idol. The man upon the bed was turned to stone, save the froth, which pulsated.

In the final struggle, terror will fight the inevitable. The little man roared maniacal curses and, rushing again to the window, began to throw various articles at the specter.

A mug, a plate, a knife, a fork, all crashed or clanged on the ground, but the song of the specter continued. The bowl of beef-tea followed. As it struck the ground the phantom ceased its cry.

The men in the chamber sank limply against the walls, with the unearthly wail still ringing in their ears and the fear unfaded from their eyes. They waited again.

The little man felt his nerves vibrate. Destruction was better than another wait. He grasped a candle and, going to the window, held it over his head and looked out.

"Ho!" he said.

His companions crawled to the window and peered out with him.

"He's eatin' the beef-tea," said the slate-colored man, faintly.

"The damn dog was hungry," said the pudgy man.

"There's your phantom," said the little man to the pudgy man.

On the bed, the old man lay dead. Without, the specter was wagging its tail.

# KILLING HIS BEAR

*A Winter Tragedy with Three Actors*

In a field of snow some green pines huddled together and sang in quavers as the wind whirled among the gullies and ridges. Icicles dangled from the trees' beards, and fine dusts of snow lay upon their brows. On the ridge-top a dismal choir of hemlocks crooned over one that had fallen. The dying sun created a dim purple and flame-colored tumult on the horizon's edge and then sank until level crimson beams struck the trees. As the red rays retreated, armies of shadows stole forward. A gray, ponderous stillness came heavily in the steps of the sun. A little man stood

under the quavering pines. He was muffled to the nose in fur and
wool, and a hideous cap was pulled tightly over his ears. His
cold and impatient feet had stamped a small platform of hard
snow beneath him. A black-barreled rifle lay in the hollow of
his arm. His eyes, watery from incessant glaring, swept over the
snowfields in front of him. His body felt dumb and bloodless,
and soft curses came forth and froze on the icy wind. The
shadows crept about his feet until he was merely a blurred
blackness, with keen eyes.

Off over the ridges, through the tangled sounds of night,
came the yell of a hound on the trail. It pierced the ears of the
little man and made his blood swim in his veins. His eyes
eagerly plunged at the wall of thickets across the stone field,
but he moved not a finger or foot. Save his eyes, he was frozen to
a statue. The cry of the hound grew louder and louder, then
passed away to a faint yelp, then still louder. At first it had a
strange vindictiveness and bloodthirstiness in it. Then it grew
mournful as the wailing of a lost thing, as, perhaps, the dog
gained on a fleeing bear. A hound, as he nears large game, has
the griefs of the world on his shoulders, and his baying tells of
the approach of death. He is sorry he came.

The long yells thrilled the little man. His eyes gleamed and
grew small, and his body stiffened to intense alertness. The
trees kept up their crooning, and the light in the west faded to
a dull red splash, but the little man's fancy was fixed on the
panting, foam-splattered hound, cantering with his hot nose to
the ground in the rear of the bear, which runs as easily and as
swiftly as a rabbit, through brush, timber, and swale. Swift
pictures of himself in a thousand attitudes under a thousand
combinations of circumstances, killing a thousand bears, passed
panoramically through him.

The yell of the hound grew until it smote the little man like a call to battle. He leaned forward, and the second finger of his right hand played a low, nervous pat-pat on the trigger of his rifle. The baying grew fierce and bloodcurdling for a moment, then the dog seemed to turn directly toward the little man, and the notes again grew wailing and mournful. It was a hot trail.

The little man, with nerves tingling and blood throbbing, remained in the shadows like a fantastic bronze figure with jeweled eyes swaying sharply in its head. Occasionally he thought he could hear the branches of the bushes in front swish together. Then silence would come again.

The hound breasted the crest of the ridge, a third of a mile away, and suddenly his full-toned cry rolled over the tangled thickets to the little man. The bear must be very near. The little man kept so still and listened so tremendously that he could hear his blood surge in his veins. All at once he heard a swish-swish in the bushes. His rifle was at his shoulder and he sighted uncertainly along the front of the thicket. The swish of the bushes grew louder. In the rear the hound was mourning over a warm scent.

The thicket opened and a great bear, indistinct and vague in the shadows, bounded into the little man's view and came terrifically across the open snowfield. The little man stood like an image. The bear did not shamble nor wobble; there was no awkwardness in his gait; he ran like a frightened kitten. It would be an endless chase for the lithe-limbed hound in the rear.

On he came, directly toward the little man. The animal heard only the crying behind him. He knew nothing of the thing with death in its hands standing motionless in the shadows before him.

Slowly the little man changed his aim until it rested where the head of the approaching shadowy mass must be. It was a wee motion, made with steady nerves and a soundless swaying of

the rifle barrel; but the bear heard, or saw, and knew. The
animal whirled swiftly and started in a new direction with an
amazing burst of speed. Its side was toward the little man now.
His rifle barrel was searching swiftly over the dark shape.
Under the foreshoulder was the place. A chance to pierce the
heart, sever an artery, or pass through the lungs. The little man
saw swirling fur over his gun barrel. The earth faded to nothing.
Only space and the game, the aim and the hunter. Mad
emotions, powerful to rock worlds, hurled through the little
man, but did not shake his tiniest nerve.

When the rifle cracked, it shook his soul to a profound depth.
Creation rocked and the bear stumbled.

The little man sprang forward with a roar. He scrambled
hastily in the bear's track. The splash of red, now dim, threw a
faint, timid beam of a kindred shade on the snow. The little man
bounded in the air.

"Hit!" he yelled, and ran on. Some hundreds of yards forward he came to a dead bear with his nose in the snow. Blood
was oozing from a wound under the shoulder, and the snow about
was sprinkled with blood. A mad froth lay in the animal's
open mouth, and his limbs were twisted from agony.

The little man yelled again and sprang forward, waving his
hat as if he were leading the cheering of thousands. He ran up
and kicked the ribs of the bear. Upon his face was the smile of
the successful lover.

# AN EXPLOSION
# OF SEVEN BABIES

*A Sullivan County Sketch*

A LITTLE man was sweating and swearing his way through an intricate forest. His hat was pushed indignantly to the far rear of his head and upon his perspiring features there was a look of conscious injury.

Suddenly he perceived ahead of him a high stone wall against which waves of bushes surged. The little man fought his way to the wall and looked over it.

A brown giantess was working in a potato patch. Upon a bench, under the eaves of a worn-out house, seven babies were wailing and rubbing their stomachs.

"Ho!" said the little man to himself. He stood, observant, for a few moments. Then he climbed painfully over the wall and came to a stand in the potato patch. His eyes wandered to the seven babies wailing and rubbing their stomachs. Their mournful music fascinated him.

"Madam," he said, as he took off his hat and bowed, "I have unfortunately lost my way. Could you direct . . ." He suddenly concluded: "Great Scott!"

He had turned his eyes from the seven babies to the brown giantess and saw upon her face the glare of a tigress. Her fingers were playing convulsively over her hoe handle, and the muscles of her throat were swollen and wriggling. Her eyes were glowing with fury. She came forward with the creeping motion of an animal about to spring.

The little man gave a backward leap. Tremendous astonishment enwrapped him and trepidation showed in his legs.

"G-good heavens, madam," he stuttered. He threw up one knee and held his spread fingers before his face. His mouth was puckered to an amazed whistle.

The giantess stood before him, her hands upon her hips, her lips curled in a snarl. She followed closely as the little man retreated backward step by step toward the fence, his eyes staring in bewilderment.

"For the love of Mike, madam, what ails you?" he spluttered.

He saw here an avenger. Wherefore he knew not, but he momentarily expected to be smitten to a pulp.

"Beast!" roared the giantess, suddenly. She reached forth and grasped the arm of the palsied little man, who cast a despairing glance at the high stone wall.

She twisted him about and then, raising a massive arm, pointed to the row of seven babies, who, as if they had gotten a cue, burst out like a brass band.

"Well, what the devil . . ." roared the little man.

"Beast!" howled the giantess, "It made'm sick! They ate ut! That dum fly-paper!"

The babies began to frantically beat their stomachs with their fists.

"Villain!" shrieked the giantess. The little man felt the winding fingers crush the flesh and bone of his arm. The giantess began to roar like a dragon. She bent over and braced herself. Then her iron arms forced the little man to his knees.

He knew he was going to be eaten. "Gawd," he moaned.

He arrived at the critical stage of degradation. He would resist. He touched some hidden spring in his being and went off like a firework. The man became a tumult. Every muscle in his body he made perform a wriggling contortion. The giantess plunged forward and kneaded him as if he were bread unbaked.

From over the stone wall came the swishing sound of moving bushes, unheard by the combatants. Presently the face of a pudgy man, tranquil in its wrinkles, appeared. Amazement instantly smote him in his tracks and he hung heavily to the stones.

From the potato patch arose a cloud of dust, pregnant with curses. In it he could dimly see the little man in a state of revolution. His legs flashed in the air like a pin wheel. The pudgy man stared with gleaming eyes at the kaleidoscope. He climbed upon the wall to get a better view. Some bellowing animal seemed to have his friend in its claws.

It soon became evident to the little man that he could not eternally revolve and kick in such a manner. He felt his blood begin to dry up and his muscles turn to paste. Those talons were squeezing his life away. His mangled arms were turning weak. He was about to be subdued.

But here the pudgy man, in his excitement, performed the feat of his life. He fell off the wall, giving an involuntary shout, and landed with a flop in the potato patch.

The brown giantess snarled. She hurled the little man from her and turned, with a toss of her disheveled locks, to face a new foe. The pudgy man quaked miserably and yelled an unintelligible explanation or apology or prayer. The brow of the giantess was black, and she strode with ferocious menace toward him.

The little man had fallen in a chaotic mass among the potato hills. He struggled to his feet. Somehow, his blood was hot in his veins, and he started to bristle courageously in reinforcement of his friend. But suddenly he changed his mind and made off at a high speed, leaving the pudgy man to his fate.

His unchosen course lay directly toward the seven babies who, in their anxiety to view the combat, had risen from the bench and were standing ready as a Roman populace to signify the little man's death by rubbing their stomachs. Intent upon the struggle, they had forgotten to howl.

But when they perceived the headlong charge of the little man, they, as a unit, exploded. It was like the sudden clang of an alarm bell to the giantess. She wheeled from the pudgy man, who climbed the wall, fell off in his haste into the bushes on the other side, and, later, allowed but the top of his head to appear over the top of it.

The giantess perceived the little man about to assault her seven babies, whose mouths were in a state of eruption. She howled, grabbed a hoe from the ground, and pursued.

The little man shied from the protesting babies and ran like a greyhound. He flung himself over a high fence. Then he waited. Curiosity held him. He had been mopped and dragged, punched and pounded, bitten and scratched. He wished to know why.

The brown giantess, mad with rage, crashed against the fence. She shook her huge fist at the little man.

"Drat yeh!" she roared.

She began to climb the fence. It is not well to behold a woman climb a fence. The little man yelled and ran off.

He stumbled and tore through a brush lot and bounced terrifically into the woods. As he halted to get breath, he heard, above the sound of the wind laughing in the trees, a final explosion by the seven babies, as, perhaps, they perceived the brown giantess returning empty-handed to the worn-out house.

As the little man went on into the woods, he perceived a crouching figure with terror-gleaming eyes. He whistled and drew near it. Directly, the little man, bedraggled, dirt-stained, bloody, and amazed, confronted the pudgy man, perspiring, limp, dusty, and astonished. They gazed at each other profoundly.

Finally the little man broke the silence.

"Devilish mysterious business," he said, slowly. The pudgy man had a thousand questions in his eyes.

"What in Heaven's name, Billie . . ." he blurted.

The little man waved his hand. "Don't ask me. I don't know anything about it."

"What?"

"No more'n a rabbit. She said something about fly-paper and the kids, that's all I know."

The pudgy man drew a long breath. "Great Lord," he said. They sat down on a log and thought.

At last, the little man got up and yawned. "I can't make head nor tail of the bloomin' business," he said wearily. They walked slowly off through the day-gloom of the woods. "I wish she hadn't called me a beast. I didn't like that," added the little man, musingly, after a time.

In a shady spot on a highway, they found their two companions, who were lazily listening to a short stranger who was holding forth at some length and with apparent enthusiasm. At the approach of the little man and the pudgy man, the short man turned to them with a smile.

"Gentlemen," he said, "I have here a wonder of the age, which I wish to present to your intelligent notice. Smithers' Eternal Fly Annihilating Paper is . . ."

The little man frothed at the mouth and cursed. Before his comrades could intervene he sprang forward and kicked the short man heavily in the stomach.

# A TENT IN AGONY

*A Sullivan County Sketch*

Four men once came to a wet place in the roadless forest to fish.
They pitched their tent fair upon the brow of a pine-clothed
ridge of riven rocks whence a boulder could be made to crash
through the brush and whirl past the trees to the lake below.
On fragrant hemlock boughs they slept the sleep of unsuccessful
fishermen, for upon the lake alternately the sun made them

lazy and the rain made them wet. Finally they ate the last bit
of bacon and smoked and burned the last fearful and wonderful
hoecake.

Immediately a little man volunteered to stay and hold the
camp while the remaining three should go the Sullivan county
miles to a farmhouse for supplies. They gazed at him dismally.
"There's only one of you—the devil make a twin," they said in
parting malediction and disappeared down the hill in the
known direction of a distant cabin. When it came night and the
hemlocks began to sob, they had not returned. The little man
sat close to his companion, the campfire, and encouraged it with
logs. He puffed fiercely at a heavily-built brier and regarded a
thousand shadows which were about to assault him. Suddenly
he heard the approach of the unknown, crackling the twigs and
rustling the dead leaves. The little man arose slowly to his feet;
his clothes refused to fit his back; his pipe dropped from his
mouth; his knees smote each other. "Hah!" he bellowed hoarsely
in menace. A growl replied, and a bear paced into the light of
the fire. The little man supported himself upon a sapling and
regarded his visitor.

The bear was evidently a veteran and a fighter, for the black
of his coat had become tawny with age. There was confidence in
his gait and arrogance in his small, twinkling eyes. He rolled
back his lips and disclosed his white teeth. The fire magnified
the red of his mouth. The little man had never before confronted the terrible, and he could not wrest it from his breast.
"Hah!" he roared. The bear interpreted this as the challenge of
a gladiator. He approached warily. As he came near, the boots
of fear were suddenly upon the little man's feet. He cried out
and then darted around the campfire. "Ho!" said the bear to
himself, "this thing won't fight—it runs. Well, suppose I catch
it." So upon his features there fixed the animal look of going—

somewhere. He started intensely around the campfire. The little man shrieked and ran furiously. Twice around they went.

The hand of heaven sometimes falls heavily upon the righteous. The bear gained.

In desperation the little man flew into the tent. The bear stopped and sniffed at the entrance. He scented the scent of many men. Finally he ventured in.

The little man crouched in a distant corner. The bear advanced, creeping, his blood burning, his hair erect, his jowls dripping. The little man yelled and rustled clumsily under the flap at the end of the tent. The bear snarled awfully and made a jump and a grab at his disappearing game. The little man, now without the tent, felt a tremendous paw grab his coat-tails. He squirmed and wriggled out of his coat, like a schoolboy in the hands of an avenger. The bear howled triumphantly and jerked the coat into the tent and took two bites, a punch, and a hug before he discovered his man was not in it. Then he grew not very angry, for a bear on a spree is not a black-haired pirate. He is merely a hoodlum. He lay down on his back, took the coat on his four paws and began to play uproariously with it. The most appalling, blood-curdling whoops and yells came to where the little man was crying in a tree-top and froze his blood. He moaned a little speech meant for a prayer and clung convulsively to the bending branches. He gazed with tearful wistfulness at where his comrade, the campfire, was giving dying flickers and crackles. Finally, there was a roar from the tent which eclipsed all roars, a snarl which it seemed would shake the stolid silence of the mountain and cause it to shrug its granite shoulders. The little man quaked and shriveled to a grip and a pair of eyes. In the glow of the embers he saw the white tent quiver and fall with a crash. The bear's merry play had disturbed the center-pole and brought a chaos of canvas about his head.

Now the little man became the witness of a mighty scene. The tent began to flounder. It took flopping strides in the direction of the lake. Marvelous sounds came from within— rips and tears, and great groans and pants. The little man went into giggling hysterics.

The entangled monster failed to extricate himself before he had frenziedly walloped the tent to the edge of the mountain. So it came to pass that three men, clambering up the hill with bundles and baskets, saw their tent approaching.

It seemed to them like a white-robed phantom pursued by hornets. Its moans riffled the hemlock twigs.

The three men dropped their bundles and scurried to one side, their eyes gleaming with fear. The canvas avalanche swept past them. They leaned, faint and dumb, against trees and listened, their blood stagnant. Below them it struck the base of a great pine tree, where it writhed and struggled. The three watched its convolutions a moment and then started terrifically for the top of the hill. As they disappeared, the bear cut loose with a mighty effort. He cast one disheveled and agonized look at the white thing, and then started wildly for the inner recesses of the forest.

The three fear-stricken individuals ran to the rebuilt fire. The little man reposed by it calmly smoking. They sprang at him and overwhelmed him with interrogations. He contemplated darkness and took a long, pompous puff. "There's only one of me—and the devil made a twin," he said.

# THE CRY OF A HUCKLEBERRY
# PUDDING

*A Dim Study of Camping Experiences*

A GREAT blaze wavered redly against the blackness of the night in the pines. Before the eyes of his expectant companions, a little man moved with stately dignity as the creator of a huckleberry pudding.

"I know how to make'm," he said in a confident voice, "just exactly right."

The others looked at him with admiration as they sat down to eat.

After a time, a pudgy man whose spoon was silent, said: "I don't like this much."

"What?" cried the little man, threateningly.

"I don't seem to get on with it," said the pudgy man. He

looked about for support in the faces of his companions. "I don't like it, somehow," he added slowly.

"Fool!" roared the little man, furiously. "You're mad because you didn't make it. I never saw such a beast."

The pudgy man wrapped himself in a great dignity. He glanced suggestingly at the plates of the two others. They were intact.

"Ho," cried the little man, "you're all idiots."

He saw that he must vindicate his work. He must eat it. He sat before them and, with ineffable bliss lighting his countenance, ate all of the huckleberry pudding. Then he laid aside his plate, lighted his pipe, and addressed his companions as unappreciative blockheads.

The pipe, the fire, and the song of the pines soothed him after a time, and he puffed tranquilly. The four men sat staring vacantly at the blaze until the spirits of the tent at the edge of the fire circle, in drowsy voices, began to call them. Their thoughts became heavily fixed on the knee-deep bed of hemlock. One by one they arose, knocked ashes from their pipes, and treading softly to the open flaps, disappeared. Alone, the campfire spluttered valiantly for a time, opposing its music to the dismal crooning of the trees that accented the absence of things congenial and alive. A curious moon peered through locked branches at imperturbable bundles of blankets which lay in the shadows of the tent.

The fragrant blackness of the early night passed away, and gray ghost-mists came winding slowly up from the marshes and stole among the wet tree trunks. Wavering leaves dotted with dewdrops glowed in a half-light of impending dawn. From the tent came sounds of heavy sleeping. The bundles of blankets clustered on the hemlock twigs.

Suddenly from off in the thickets of the gloom, there came a cry. It seemed to crash on the tent. It smote the bundles of blankets. There was instant profound agitation, a whirling chaos of coverings, legs, and arms; then, heads appeared. The men had heard the voice of the unknown, crying in the wilderness, and it made their souls quaver.

They had slumbered through the trees' song of loneliness and the lay of isolation of the mountain grass. Hidden frogs had muttered ominously since nightfall, and distant owls, undoubtedly perched on lofty branches and silhouetted by the moon, had hooted. There had been an endless hymning by leaves, blades, and unseen live things, through which these men, who adored Wagner, had slept.

But a false note in the sounds of night had convulsed them. A strange tune had made them writhe.

The cry of the unknown instantly awoke them to terror. It is mightier than the war yell of the dreadful, because the dreadful may be definite. But this whoop strikes greater fear from hearts because it tells of formidable mouths and great, grasping claws that live in impossibility. It is the chant of a phantom force which imagination declares invincible, and awful to the sight.

In the tent, eyes aglitter with terror gazed into eyes. Knees softly smote each other, and lips trembled.

The pudgy man gave vent to a tremendous question. "What was that?" he whispered.

The others made answer with their blanched faces. The group, waiting in the silence that followed their awakening, wriggled their legs in the agony of fright. There was a pause which extended through space. Comets hung and worlds waited. Their thoughts shot back to that moment when they had started upon the trip, and they were filled with regret that it had been.

"Oh, goodness, what was that?" repeated the pudgy man, intensely.

Suddenly, their faces twitched and their fingers turned to wax. The cry was repeated. Its burden caused the men to huddle together like drowning kittens. They watched the banshees of the fog drifting lazily among the trees. They saw eyes in the gray obscurity. They heard a thousand approaching footfalls in the rustling of the dead leaves. They groveled.

Then, they heard the unknown stride to and fro in the forest, giving calls, weighted with challenge, that could make cities hearing, fear. Roars went to the ends of earth, and snarls that would appall armies turned the men in the tent to a moaning mass with forty eyes. The challenges changed to wailings as of a fever-torn soul. Later, there came snorts of anger that sounded cruel, like the noise of a rampant bull on a babies' playground. Later still, howls, as from an abandoned being, strangling in the waters of trouble.

"Great Scott!" roared the pudgy man, "I can't stand this."

He wriggled to his feet and tottered out to the dying fire. His companions followed. They had reached the cellar of fear. They were now resolved to use weapons on the great destruction. They would combat the inevitable. They peered among the trees, wherefrom a hundred assaulting shadows came. The unknown was shrieking.

Of a sudden, the pudgy man screamed like a wounded animal.

"It's got Billie," he howled. They discovered that the little man was gone.

To listen or to wait is the most tense of occupations. In their absorption they had not seen that a comrade was missing.

Instantly, their imaginations perceived his form in the clutch of a raging beast.

"Come on," shouted the pudgy man. They grasped bludgeons

and rushed valiantly into the darkness. They stumbled from gloom to gloom in a mad rush for their friend's life. The keynote of terror kept clanging in their ears and guided their scrambling feet. Tangled thickets tripped them. Saplings buffeted heroically, and stones turned away. Branches smote their heads so that it appeared as if lightning had flapped its red wings in their faces.

Once, the pudgy man stopped. The unknown was just ahead.

The dim lights of early dawn came charging through the forest. The gray and black of mist and shadow retreated before crimson beams that had advanced to the tree-tops.

The men came to a stand, waving their heads to glance down the aisles of the wilderness.

"There he is," shouted the pudgy man. The party, rushing forward, came upon the form of the little man, quivering at the foot of a tree. His blood seemed to be turned to salt. From out his wan, white face his eyes shone with a blue light. "Oh, thunderation," he moaned. "Oh, thunderation."

"What!" cried his friends. Their voices shook with anxiety.

"Oh, thunderation," repeated he.

"For the love of Mike, tell us, Billie," cried the pudgy man, "what is the matter."

"Oh, thunderation," wailed the little man. Suddenly he rolled about on the ground and gave vent to a howl that rolled and pealed over the width of the forest. Its tones told of death and fear and unpaid debts. It clamored like a song of forgotten war, and died away to the scream of a maiden. The pleadings of fire-surrounded children mingled with the calls of wave-threatened sailors. Two barbaric tribes clashed together on a sunburnt plain; a score of bareknee'd clansmen crossed claymores amid gray rocks; a woman saw a lover fall; a dog was stabbed in an alley; a steel knight bit dust with bloody mouth; a savage saw a burning home.

The rescuing party leaned weakly against trees. After the little man had concluded, there was a silence.

Finally, the pudgy man advanced. He struggled with his astonished tongue for a moment. "Do you mean to say, Billie," he said at last, "that all that tangled chaos emanated from you?"

The little man made no reply, but heaved about on the ground, moaning: "Oh, thunderation."

The three men contemplating him suddenly felt themselves swell with wrath. They had been terrorized to no purpose. They had expected to be eaten. They were not. The fact maddened them. The pudgy man voiced the assembly.

"You infernal little jay, get up off'n the ground and come on," he cried. "You make me sick."

"Oh, thunderation," replied the little man.

The three men began to berate him. They turned into a babble of wrath.

"You scared us to death."

"What do you wanta holler that way for?"

"You're a bloomin' nuisance. For heaven's sake, what are you yellin' about?"

The little man staggered to his feet. Anger took hold of him. He waved his arms eloquently.

"That pudding, you fools," he cried.

His companions paused and regarded him.

"Well," said the pudgy man, eventually, "what in blazes did you eat it for then?"

"Well, I didn't know," roared the other, "I didn't know that it was that way."

"You shouldn't have eaten it, anyhow. There was the sin. You shouldn't have eaten it anyway."

"But I didn't know," shouted the little man.

"You should have known," they stormed. "You've made idiots of us. You scared us to death with your hollerin'."

As he reeled toward the camp, they followed him, railing like fishwives.

The little man turned at bay.

"Exaggerated fools," he yelled. "Fools, to apply no salve but moral teaching to a man with the stomach-ache."

# THE HOLLER TREE
*A Sullivan County Sketch*

As THEY went along a narrow woodpath, the little man accidentally stumbled against the pudgy man. The latter was carrying a basket of eggs, and he became angry.

"Look out, can't you! Do you wanta break all these eggs? Walk straight—what's the matter with you?" he said and passed on.

The little man saved his balance with difficulty. He had to keep from spilling a pail of milk. "T'blazes with your old eggs," he called out.

The pudgy man spoke over his shoulder. "Well, you needn't have any when we get to camp, then," he said.

"Who wants any of your infernal old eggs. Keep your infernal old eggs," replied the little man.

The four men trudged on into the forest until presently the little man espied a dead tree. He paused. "Look at that tree," he said.

They scrutinized it. It was a tall, gaunt relic of a pine that stood like a yellow warrior still opposing an aged form to blows in storm-battles.

"I bet it's got lots of nests in it and all sorts of things like that," murmured the little man. The pudgy man scoffed. "Oh, fudge," he said.

"Well, I bet it has," asserted the other.

The four men put down their loads of provisions and stood around and argued.

"Yes, I bet it's a cornerstone with an almanac in it and a census report and a certified list of the pew-holders," said the pudgy man to the little man.

The latter swore for some time. "Put up even money," he demanded in conclusion. "Put up even money."

"Look out—you'll kick over the eggs," replied the pudgy man.

"Well, put up even money. You daren't."

The pudgy man scornfully kicked a stone. "Oh, fudge. How you going to prove it? Tell me that."

The little man thought. "Well," he said, eventually, "I'll climb up. That's how."

The pudgy man looked at the tree and at the little man. He

thought.

"I'll cover you," he suddenly decided.

The little man laid down his pipe, tightened his belt, and went off and looked at the tree.

"Well . . ." he began, coming back.

"Go on and climb it," said the pudgy man. "You said you'd climb it."

The little man went off and looked at the tree again. "Well, I will," he said, finally. The pudgy man giggled. The little man tightened his belt more. He approached and put both arms around the tree.

"Say," he said, turning round. "You—I . . ."

"Go on and climb it," interrupted the pudgy man. "You said you'd climb it."

The little man began to climb schoolboy fashion. He found many difficulties. The wood crumbled and rubbed into his clothes. He felt smeared. Besides, there was a horrible strain upon his legs.

When about half way, he ceased wriggling and turned his head cautiously. "Say . . ."

The three men had been regarding him intently. They then burst out. "Go on! Go on! You've got that far—what's the use of stopping? I believe you're gettin' scared! Oh, my!"

He swore and continued up. Several times he seemed about to fall in a lump. The three below held their breath.

Once, he paused to deliver an oration and forgot his grip for a moment. It was near being fatal.

At last, he reached the top. "Well?" said the pudgy man. The little man gazed about him. There was a somber sea of pines, rippling in a wind. Far away, there was a little house, and two yellow fields.

"Fine scenery up here," he murmured.

"Oh, bother," said the pudgy man. "Where's your nests and all that? That's what I wanta know."

The little man peered down the hollow trunk. "They're in there."

The pudgy man grinned. "How do you know?"

The little man looked down the hole again. "It's all dark," he said.

The pudgy man complacently lit a fresh pipe. "Certainly, it is," he remarked. "You look great up there, don't you? What you goin' to do now, eh?"

The little man balanced himself carefully on the ragged edge and looked thoughtfully at the hole. "Well, I might slide down," he said in a doubtful voice.

"That's it," cried the other. "That's what you wanta do! Slide down!"

"Well," said the little man, "it looks pretty dangerous."

"Oh, I see! You're afraid!"

"I aint!"

"Yes, you are, too! Else why don't you slide down?"

"Well, how th' devil do I know but what something's down there?" shouted the little man in a rage.

His companion replied with scorn. "Pooh! Nothin' but a hollow tree! You're afraid of the dark!"

"You must take me for a fool! What th' blazes do I wanta be slidin' down every hollow tree I see for?"

"Well, you climbed up, didn't you? What are you up there for? You can't find your little nests and things just settin' there an' cursin', can you? You're afraid, I bet!"

"You make . . ."

"Oh, yes, you are. You know you are."

The little man flung his legs over and slid down until only his head and his gripping fingers appeared. He seemed to be feeling about with his feet.

"There's nothing to climb down with," he said, finally.

"Certainly not. Did you hope for a stairway? You're afraid."

The little man's face flushed and his eyes grew like beads. He glared from out of the hole.

"I am not, you big . . ."

"Oh, yes, you are. Anyone can see it."

"Thunderation, you're th' . . ."

"Oh, come, Billie, either climb down th' outside or slide down th' inside. There's no use of you sittin' up there, you know, if you ain't going to do something. You're afraid, that's what."

"I tell you I ain't. What th' devil . . .?"

"Oh, yes, you are, too. You're pale with fright, Billie. We can see it down here. Oh, my! I'm surprised."

The little man raised a fist. "Thunder and blazes . . ."

He vanished down the hole.

The wood had crumbled and broken under the strain of the one hand. Hollow sounds of scratchings and thumpings came to the ears of his three companions. In agitation they ran about the vibrating trunk and called to their comrade in many voices. They were fearful he had met his time.

Presently, they heard a muffled noise of swearing. They listened. Down near the ground, the little man was cursing under forced draft. The old tree shook like a smokestack.

The pudgy man approached and put near his ear.

"Billie!"

"What?"

"Are you inside the tree?"

The little man began to kick and clamor. His voice came in a dull roar. "Certainly I'm inside the tree. Where th' devil did you suppose I was? What th' . . .?"

His voice died away in smothered thunder.

"Well, but, Billie," asked the pudgy man anxiously, "how you going to get out?"

The little man began to rage again. "What a fool you are. I don't know how I'm going to get out. Don't suppose I've got plans made already, do you?"

"Well, I guess you'll have to climb," mused the pudgy man. "That's the only way, and you can't stay in there forever, you know."

The little man made some efforts. There was a sound of rending clothes. Presently he ceased.

"It's no go," he announced.

The three men sat down and debated upon theories.

Finally the little man began to roar at them and kick his prison wall. "Think I wanta stay in here while you fellows hold arguments for a couple of hours? Why th' thunder don't you do something instead of talking so much? What do you think I am anyway?"

The pudgy man approached the tree. "You might as well keep quiet," he said in a grim voice. "You're in there and you might as well keep quiet . . ."

The little man began to swear.

"Stop your howling," angrily cried the pudgy man. "There's no use of howlin'."

"I won't! It's your fault I'm in here. If it hadn't been for you, I wouldn't 'a climbed up."

"Well, I didn't make you fall down inside, anyway. You did that yourself."

"I didn't either. You made me tumble, old pudgkins. If you had minded your own business it would have been all right. It's your stupidity that's got me in here."

"It was your own, you little fool. I . . ."

The little man began to rave and wriggle. The pudgy man went very near to the tree and stormed. They had a furious quarrel. The eloquence of the little man caused some tremors in the tree, and presently it began to sway gently.

Suddenly, the pudgy man screamed. "You're pushin' th' tree over on me." He started away. The trunk trembled and tottered and began to fall. It seemed like a mighty blow aimed by the wrathful little man at the head of the fleeing pudgy man.

The latter bounded, light as a puff ball, over the ground. His face was white with terror. He turned an agonized somersault into a thicket as the tree, with a splintering cry, crashed near his heels. He lay in a bush and trembled.

The little man's legs were wagging plaintively from the other end of the trunk. The two remaining men rushed forward with cries of alarm and began to tug at them. The little man came forth, finally. He was of deep bronze hue from a coating of wet dead wood. A soft bed of it came with him. They helped him to his feet. He felt his shoulders and legs with an air of anxiety. After a time, he rubbed the crumbles from his eyes and began to stagger and swear softly.

Suddenly, he perceived the pudgy man lying pale in the bush. He limped over to him.

The pudgy man was moaning. "Lord, it just missed me by 'bout an inch."

The little man thoughtfully contemplated his companion. Presently, a smile was born at the corners of his mouth and grew until it wreathed his face. The pudgy man cursed in an unhappy vein as he was confronted by the little man's grins.

The latter seemed about to deliver an oration, but, instead, he turned and, picking up his pail of milk, started away. He paused once and looked back. He pointed with his forefinger.

"There's your eggs—under the tree," he said.

He resumed his march down the forest pathway. His stride was that of a proud grenadier.

# THE MESMERIC MOUNTAIN

*A Tale of Sullivan County*

On the brow of a pine-plumed hillock there sat a little man with his back against a tree. A venerable pipe hung from his mouth, and smoke-wreaths curled slowly skyward. He was muttering to himself with his eyes fixed on an irregular black opening in the green wall of forest at the foot of the hill. Two vague wagon ruts led into the shadows. The little man took his pipe in his hands and addressed the listening pines.

"I wonder what the devil it leads to," said he.

A gray, fat rabbit came lazily from a thicket and sat in the opening. Softly stroking his stomach with his paw, he looked at the little man in a thoughtful manner. The little man threw a stone, and the rabbit blinked and ran through an opening. Green, shadowy portals seemed to close behind him.

The little man started. "He's gone down that roadway," he said with ecstatic mystery to the pines. He sat a long time and contemplated the door to the forest. Finally, he arose, and awakening his limbs, started away. But he stopped and looked back.

"I can't imagine what it leads to," muttered he. He trudged over the brown mats of pine needles to where, in a fringe of laurel, a tent was pitched and merry flames caroused about some logs. A pudgy man was fuming over a collection of tin dishes. He came forward and waved a plate furiously in the little man's face.

"I've washed the dishes for three days. What do you think I am . . ." He ended a red oration with a roar: "Damned if I do it any more."

The little man gazed dim-eyed away. "I've been wonderin' what it leads to."

"What?"

"That road out yonder. I've been wonderin' what it leads to. Maybe some discovery or something," said the little man.

The pudgy man laughed. "You're an idiot. It leads to ol' Jim Boyd's over on the Lumberland Pike."

"Ho!" said the little man. "I don't believe that."

The pudgy man swore. "Fool, what does it lead to, then?"

"I don't know just what, but I'm sure it leads to something great or something. It looks like it."

While the pudgy man was cursing, two more men came from

obscurity with fish dangling from birch twigs. The pudgy man made an obviously herculean struggle, and a meal was prepared. As he was drinking his cup of coffee, he suddenly spilled it and swore. The little man was wandering off.

"He's gone to look at that hole," cried the pudgy man.

The little man went to the edge of the pine-plumed hillock and, sitting down, began to make smoke and regard the door to the forest. There was stillness for an hour. Compact clouds hung unstirred in the sky. The pines stood motionless, and pondering.

Suddenly the little man slapped his knee and bit his tongue. He stood up and determinedly filled his pipe, rolling his eye over the bowl to the doorway. Keeping his eyes fixed, he slid dangerously to the foot of the hillock and walked down the wagon ruts. A moment later he passed from the noise of the sunshine to the gloom of the woods.

The green portals closed, shutting out live things. The little man trudged on alone.

Tall tangled grass grew in the roadway, and the trees bent obstructing branches. The little man followed on over pine-clothed ridges and down through water-soaked swales. His shoes were cut by rocks of the mountains, and he sank ankle-deep in mud and moss of swamps. A curve just ahead lured him miles.

Finally, as he wended the side of a ridge, the road disappeared from beneath his feet. He battled with hordes of ignorant bushes on his way to knolls and solitary trees which invited him. Once he came to a tall, bearded pine. He climbed it, and perceived in the distance a peak. He uttered an ejaculation and fell out.

He scrambled to his feet and said: "That's Jones's Mountain, I guess. It's about six miles from our camp as the crow flies."

He changed his course away from the mountain, and attacked the bushes again. He climbed over great logs, golden-brown in decay, and was opposed by thickets of dark-green laurel. A brook slid through the ooze of a swamp; cedars and hemlocks hung their sprays to the edges of pools.

The little man began to stagger in his walk. After a time he stopped and mopped his brow.

"My legs are about to shrivel up and drop off," he said. " . . . Still, if I keep on in this direction, I am safe to strike the Lumberland Pike before sundown."

He dived at a clump of tag-alders and, emerging, confronted Jones's Mountain.

The wanderer sat down in a clear place and fixed his eyes on the summit. His mouth opened widely, and his body swayed at times. The little man and the peak stared in silence.

A lazy lake lay asleep near the foot of the mountain. In its bed of water-grass some frogs leered at the sky and crooned. The sun sank in red silence, and the shadows of the pines grew formidable. The expectant hush of evening, as if something were going to sing a hymn, fell upon the peak and the little man.

A leaping pickerel off on the water created a silver circle that was lost in black shadows. The little man shook himself and started to his feet, crying: "For the love of Mike, there's eyes in this mountain! I feel 'em! Eyes!"

He fell on his face.

When he looked again, he immediately sprang erect and ran. "It's comin'!"

The mountain was approaching.

The little man scurried, sobbing, through the thick growth. He felt his brain turning to water. He vanquished brambles with mighty bounds.

But after a time he came again to the foot of the mountain.

"God!" he howled, "it's been follerin' me." He groveled. Casting his eyes upward made circles swirl in his blood. "I'm shackled, I guess," he moaned.

As he felt the heel of the mountain about to crush his head, he sprang again to his feet. He grasped a handful of small stones and hurled them. "Damn you!" he shrieked loudly. The pebbles rang against the face of the mountain.

The little man then made an attack. He climbed with hands and feet wildly. Brambles forced him back and stones slid from beneath his feet. The peak swayed and tottered, and was ever about to smite with a granite arm. The summit was a blaze of red wrath.

But the little man at last reached the top. Immediately, he swaggered with valor to the edge of the cliff. His hands were scornfully in his pockets.

He gazed at the western horizon, edged sharply against a yellow sky. "Ho!" he said. "There's Boyd's house and the Lumberland Pike."

The mountain under his feet was motionless.

*Stephen Crane was a student at Syracuse University between January and June of 1891; a year later the sketches which appear in this book had been completed.*

*Melvin H. Schoberlin, who collected the stories and wrote the Introduction, lives in Phoenix, Arizona. Mr. Schoberlin is the author of* FROM CANDLES TO FOOTLIGHTS *and a book of poetry,* ROADS: AND OTHER LINES. *He is preparing a definitive biography of Stephen Crane.*

*The designer of this book is Gordon Paxson. The illustrations are by George Vander Sluis. Both of these men are faculty members of the School of Art, Syracuse University.*

*Typesetting and printing is by the Morrill Press, Fulton, New York. The body text is ten-point Scotch Roman on a twelve-point body. Scotch Roman, with its English and Scotch ancestors, has a little more color than many other types, and a crispness that makes it easily read. The paper is Warren's Olde Style furnished by the Hudson Valley Paper Company. Binding is by the Chas. H. Bohn Company.*